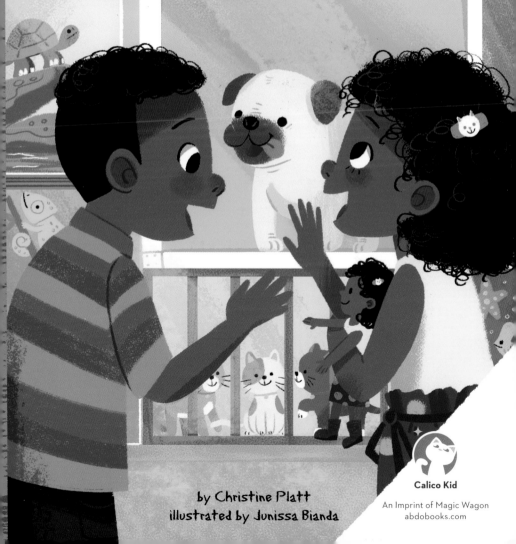

ana &
anDReW
The Perfect Pet

by Christine Platt
illustrated by Junissa Bianda

Calico Kid
An Imprint of Magic Wagon
abdobooks.com

About the Author
Christine A. Platt is an author and scholar of African and
African-American history. A beloved storyteller of the African
diaspora, Christine enjoys writing historical fiction and non-fiction
for people of all ages. You can learn more about her and her
work at christineaplatt.com.

For my friend, Ian McPherson. —CP

To my number one supporter, Krisna Aditya. —JB

abdobooks.com

Printed in the United States of America, North Mankato, Minnesota.
102019
012020

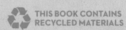

THIS BOOK CONTAINS
RECYCLED MATERIALS

Written by Christine Platt
Illustrated by Junissa Bianda
Edited by Tamara L. Britton
Art Directed by Candice Keimig

Library of Congress Control Number: 2019942372

Publisher's Cataloging-in-Publication Data

Names: Platt, Christine, author. | Bianda, Junissa, illustrator.
Title: The perfect pet / by Christine Platt ; illustrated by Junissa Bianda.
Description: Minneapolis, Minnesota : Magic Wagon, 2020. | Series: Ana & Andrew
Summary: Ana & Andrew are getting a new pet! They research different pets before choosing
    the best pet for their family. Then they pick a name for it! With the name Ana & Andrew
    choose, they learn from a famous African American that skin color does not affect a
    person's abilities.
Identifiers: ISBN 9781532136399 (lib. bdg.) | ISBN 9781644942635 (pbk.) | ISBN
    9781532136993 (ebook) | ISBN 9781532137297 (Read-to-Me ebook)
Subjects: LCSH: African American families--Juvenile fiction. | Pets--Juvenile fiction. | Pets--
    Names--Juvenile fiction. | Responsibility in children--Juvenile fiction. | Color of human
    beings--Juvenile fiction. | Ancestry--Juvenile fiction.
Classification: DDC [E]--dc23

Table of Contents

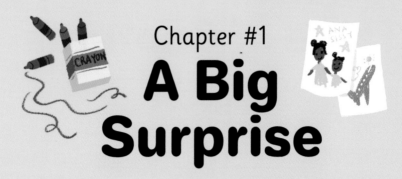

Chapter #1
A Big Surprise

One Sunday afternoon, Ana was coloring a picture of her and her favorite dolly, Sissy. Andrew was coloring a large airplane.

"You are working so nicely together," Mama encouraged.

"Thank you," Andrew said.

"Yes, me and Sissy thank you too." Ana smiled.

"In fact, Papa and I have been watching you both very closely. And we are very proud of you."

Ana and Andrew always tried their best to be good children, and good siblings to each other. They practiced playing their instruments. After school, they completed their homework. They always did their chores and cleaned up after playtime.

"We are so proud of your behavior, we have a big surprise for you," Papa said.

"Really?" Ana and Andrew looked at each other and smiled. They loved surprises.

"Yes, we think you are ready for your first pet!" Mama and Papa said excitedly.

Andrew did a wiggle dance. "Oh boy!"

Ana laughed and hugged Sissy.

Ana and Andrew had wanted a pet for a long time. They were very happy Mama and Papa thought they were responsible enough to have one.

Chapter #2
Time to Research

First, Ana and Andrew had to decide which animal would make the perfect pet.

"Mama, can we please use the computer?" Andrew asked.

"Of course," Mama said. "Having a pet is a big responsibility. You want to make sure you can take good care of whichever pet you choose."

Ana and Andrew really liked cats. Unfortunately, Papa was allergic. Still, there were plenty of pets to choose from.

Andrew searched online for different pets while Ana took notes.

Dogs were the first pets they researched. They loved playing with their neighbor's dog, Charlie! But having a pet dog was a big responsibility, especially since dogs needed to be walked twice a day or more.

"With school, music lessons, and performances, we don't have enough time to give a dog the love and attention it deserves," Andrew said.

Ana agreed and marked 'dog' off their list.

Next, Andrew researched birds. There were so many! Aside from singing, some birds could talk. Ana and Andrew even saw a video of a parrot skateboarding, which was amazing.

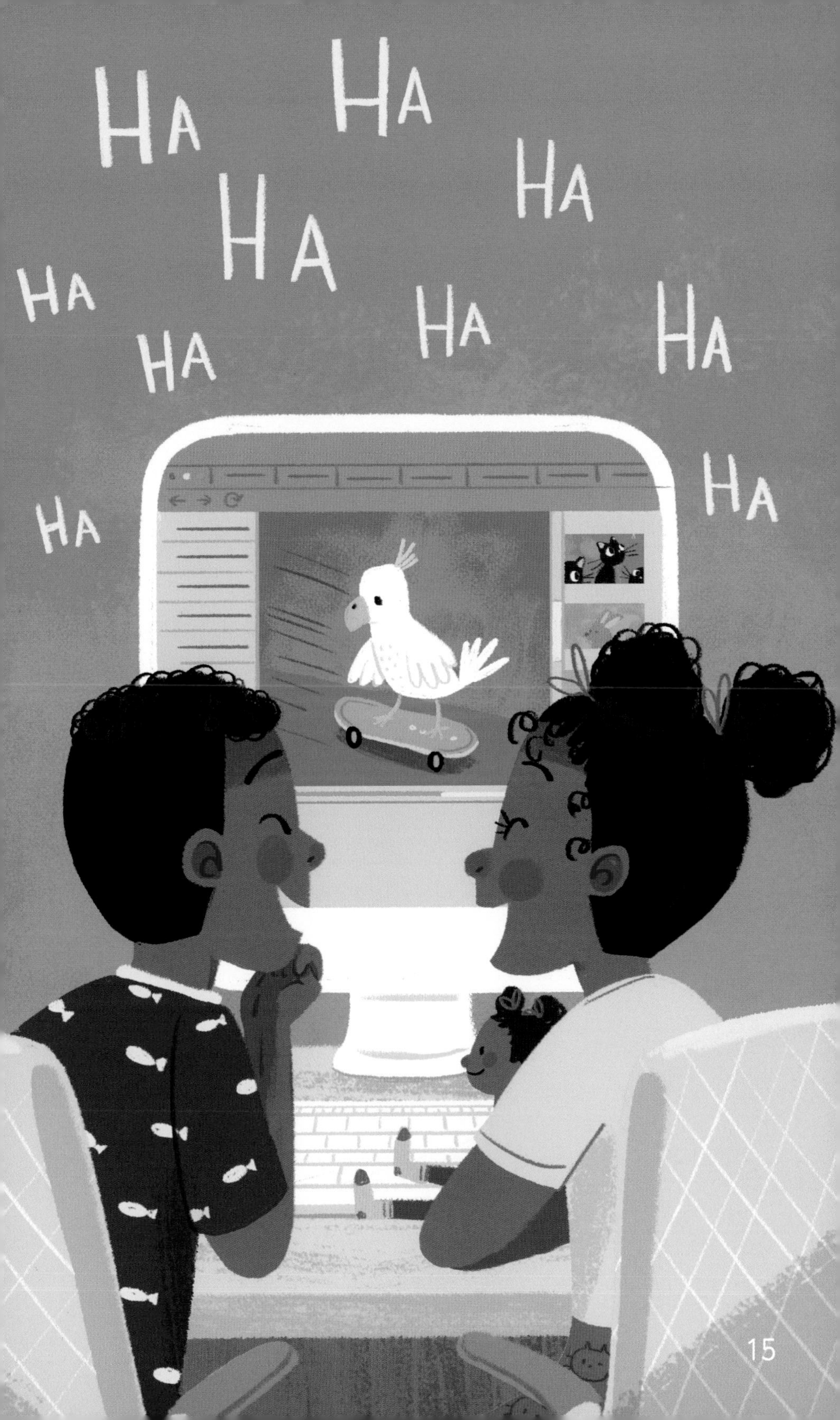
HA
HA
HA
HA
HA
HA
HA
HA
HA
HA

When Andrew started to research snakes, Ana said, "Sissy does not like snakes!"

"Does she like turtles?" Andrew asked.

"Yes, Sissy likes turtles."

After researching turtles, Andrew also researched two furry animals— hamsters and rabbits. Soon, Ana and Andrew narrowed down their choices to three animals: a bird, a hamster, or a turtle.

Chapter #3
Decisions, Decisions

"Have you made a decision?" Papa asked Ana and Andrew.

"Yes, we narrowed it down to three pets," Andrew told Mama and Papa.

"And it is going to be hard to pick one because we like them for different reasons," Ana said.

"Well, let's discuss the pros and cons for each one," Mama encouraged.

"Pros and cons?" Ana asked.

"Yes, the good things and the not-so-good things," Mama explained.

Ana read through her notes.

Birds were pretty and nice to look at. But they weren't furry and playful.

Turtles were easy to take care of. "And we can take it out of its tank and play with it," Ana said.

"But turtles move really, really slow." Andrew crawled across the living room floor in slow motion and everyone laughed.

"And what did you learn about hamsters?" Mama asked. "Aside from them not being slow, like turtles."

Hamsters were furry, which Ana and Andrew liked. They were easy to hold and cuddle with. Hamsters slept or played with their toys until their owners came home. Plus, Ana and Andrew had seen a lot of videos of kids having fun with hamsters.

"I think I know what pet we should get," Andrew said.

"Me too!" Ana hugged Sissy.

Everyone was very excited.

Chapter #4
It's Perfect!

The next Saturday, Ana and Andrew went to the pet store with their parents. The sales associate showed them where to find the hamsters.

"Look!" Ana pointed to a golden hamster running on a wheel. "It's so cute!"

"Would you like to hold him?"
The sales associate asked.

Ana and Andrew took turns
holding the soft, furry hamster.

"It's perfect!" Andrew did a wiggle dance. And when he put the hamster back in the cage, the hamster did a wiggle dance too.

"Sissy says this hamster is the one!" Ana hugged her dolly tight.